LEO'S GIFT

by

Susan Blackaby and **Joellyn Cicciarelli**

illustrated by

Carrie Schuler

To Molly Beth & Rosemary –
Share your gifts!

LOYOLAPRESS.

Leo peeked around the stairs to listen to his sister's piano lesson. He could hear Mrs. Peale keeping rhythm as Meredith picked through a Mozart sonata. Leo liked the tune. It twisted up and down and fluttered again and again along the way.

The song flowed like a spring stream, whirling and swirling around rocks and stones, a stream that finally splashed down on a bright, happy *Ta-da!*

Leo popped out of sight as Mrs. Peale packed up to leave. "The recital is the first week of December, Meredith. This piece should be ready—if you practice very hard." She slung her satchel over her shoulder and reached for the doorknob. "Like I always say, music carves a deep memory."

Piano practice *was* very hard for Meredith. Every time she needed to sit down at the piano, Meredith fussed and fumed. Today was no different.

"Children should be outside in the fresh air. I'm suffocating, Mother!" She could hear her friends shooting baskets at the playground across the street. "Absolutely suffocating!"

"Thirty minutes." Mom used her no-discussion voice.

"I will! I promise! Later?" Meredith put on her best begging face, but Mom wasn't even looking.

"Now." Mom pointed at the piano bench on her way to the kitchen. "I'm setting the timer."

Meredith slumped at the piano. Leo made a joke about Mrs. "Banana Peel." He knew how to cheer up Meredith and was always glad to see a smile tug the corner of her mouth. Leo took a chance and spoke up.

"M," he said. "Show me how to play?"

Meredith moved over to make room on the bench, and Leo hopped up.

Meredith explained the keyboard and the sets of white and black keys and how to find middle C. She explained sharps and flats. She showed Leo how to tuck his thumb under to play a scale when he ran out of fingers and how to play three keys at the same time to make a chord.

"How do you know if you're doing it right?" asked Leo.

Meredith shrugged. "It sounds wrong if you do it wrong. Piano doesn't come easily to me like basketball does, so I have to work extra hard and take lessons and practice. And believe me, there is even more than that to really getting it right. It's exhausting!"

Leo nodded. "Okay, so now play the one that sounds like water, the one with the toodle-oodles at the beginning," he said. "You know, this one."

Leo expertly played the beginning of the Mozart sonata.

"What? That's amazing!" Meredith jabbed him in the side with her elbow. "How did you do that?"

Leo wiggled his fingers. "I did what you said. I made it sound right."

Mom called from the kitchen. "Very nice, Meredith, but take it a little slower. And don't stop this time. Remember what Mrs. Peale says—music carves a deep memory."

Meredith grinned. Knowing she had finally found a way to make practice easy, she leaned in to whisper, "Play it again, Leo. But a little slower."

Leo liked how the music made him feel, wrapped inside a safe cocoon of sound. And he liked sharing his secret only with Meredith, so he made sure Mom and Dad didn't catch him.

Meredith joked that Leo made practicing a breeze,
but she could see how the music affected him when
he got a chance to play. She let him listen
to her music when they were in the car
and winked at him as he drummed out
melodies on his knees.

When basketball started the first week of
September, Meredith made the team. Leo knew he
had to wait in the corner until Meredith was ready
to walk home with him.

Meredith dribbled over to check on her brother.
"Are you okay? Did you remember all your stuff?"

Leo held up his backpack. "Yup."

"Good job, Bud. Stay put." Meredith trotted away.

But Leo didn't like the big, echoey gym, so he slipped out to find a better place to wait.

Watch me disappear, thought Leo. He climbed onto the piano bench. He plinked a few notes and immediately felt a wave of relief. He smiled as his fingers danced up and down the C scale. Then he went up five notes and played a G scale, once without a sharp and once with a sharp. Meredith was right. It sounded wrong if you did it wrong.

"Is there a person back there, or is this piano playing itself?" asked Mr. Alonzo, the music teacher. "Let me see whose face goes with that hair. Ah, yes. You must be Meredith's little brother."

Leo nodded nervously. "I'm waiting for her in here if that's okay. Basketball isn't really for me."

"Me neither." Mr. Alonzo smiled. "I'm curious. Did Meredith always have such a great jump shot?"

Leo thought, and then said, "No, but she's always had those jabby elbows. Those seem to help her."

Mr. Alonzo laughed. "I see. So Meredith had a good start with basketball because of her elbows. But then I guess she works hard, practices a lot?"

Leo nodded. "Dad says she has a special gift."

"Leo, everyone has a special gift. It's like a treasure we carry inside, a treasure we need to practice and polish and share."

Mr. Alonzo smiled at Leo. "Meredith has a gift for basketball, a treasure to share. You have one too. You don't have to worry about what it is. Just pay attention. You'll know it when you find it."

Leo thought about what his treasure might be.

"How will I know?" asked Leo.

Mr. Alonzo put his hand on his heart. "You get a feeling. A feeling that makes you want to share your gift."

Leo made a face that he hoped looked as if he understood. "Do you mind if I stay in here during practice?"

"Not at all." Mr. Alonzo winked. "I'm with the club every day anyway. I'll tell the elbow-jabbing hoopster where to find you."

On the way home, Leo asked Meredith, "Did you know that if you go up five notes, you add a black key each time?"

"What do you mean?"

"The C scale has no black keys," said Leo. "If you count up five white keys—C-D-E-F-G—and start the scale on G, you have to add a black key or it sounds wrong. And if you count up five more keys—G-A-B-C-D—and start with D, you have to add two black keys."

Meredith gave Leo a quizzical look. "How did you figure that out?"

"I used the piano in the music room. But don't worry. Mr. Alonzo says it's okay for me to be there." Leo thought about Mr. Alonzo's words. "He says if you practice and polish your gifts, then you'll want to share them with others. Maybe that would work for your recital."

Meredith groaned. "Don't remind me. Music is fine, but I just want to play basketball. Basketball practice is the best part of the week."

Pretty soon, it was the best part of Leo's week too.

Mr. Alonzo was waiting in the music room when Leo arrived. "I have something for you." He handed Leo a dictionary that was so large and heavy Leo could hardly hold it.

Leo thanked Mr. Alonzo, but he felt confused as he shuffled toward the piano bench. He set the dictionary down. He wanted to practice, but he spent some time looking up words just in case Mr. Alonzo was testing him. He looked up music words and piano words, and then he looked up *gift* and *treasure,* just in case.

gift noun \'gift\
1. a present
2. a talent, ability, a special capacity in a person

treasure noun \trea·sure\
1. any kind of resource or quality of great value
2. wealth

Mr. Alonzo came up beside him and asked, "May I?"
He closed the book.

Leo laughed as he climbed on the bench. Sitting on
the dictionary raised Leo to the perfect height for playing
anything he pleased.

Ta-da! Leo played the bright chord in Meredith's Mozart
sonata. He lifted his gaze from the keyboard, and Mr.
Alonzo gave him a thumbs-up.

And for the rest of basketball season,

Leo practiced,

and practiced,

and practiced.

On the day of Meredith's recital, Leo and his family met Mrs.
Peale at Sunnybrook Senior Home. She introduced them to her mother,
Miss Ella, who lived there in the Memory Care Unit. Leo's mom had
explained that Miss Ella no longer recognized or remembered Mrs.
Peale. Miss Ella didn't respond to their greeting. She was lost in her
own tune, softly humming the same few notes over and over.

In the community room, Christmas decorations shimmered
everywhere. At the front of the room was a concert grand piano that
gleamed like black glass, shinier than any ornament on the tree. It
was the most beautiful thing Leo had ever seen.

Leo sat beside Miss Ella during the recital. As the students played each piece, Leo felt the swirl of notes wrap around him. He looked around the audience. With each wistful waltz or sweet sonata, the audience became more calm and quiet—everyone except Miss Ella. Leo began to worry because Miss Ella was still humming. *She is missing the recital,* Leo thought. Feeling sad, Leo looked away.

His eyes landed on the angel at the top of the Christmas tree. And at that very moment, Leo knew. He knew what Miss Ella was humming, and he knew what Mrs. Peale meant when she said, "Music carves a deep memory."

After the recital, family, friends, and caregivers bustled around the refreshment table. Meredith and her friends giggled in a corner, reliving their flubby moments.

Leo wandered over to the piano. He stood on his tiptoes to peek inside, following the strings from hammer to peg.

"You." Leo jumped and turned. Miss Ella had stopped humming and was pointing at him. Her soft voice sounded like crumply tissue paper. "Play it now."

Leo grabbed a cushion and hopped onto the bench. The piano was as big as a sailboat, but the keyboard was the usual size. Leo reached out and rested his right thumb on middle C.

A tingly feeling twitched from Leo's feet to his knees. As he touched the keys, the feeling got bigger and fizzier and stopped to swirl around in his tummy before it bubbled up and burst into a grin.

It was a good feeling. It was a strong feeling. It was that feeling.

And Mr. Alonzo was right. Leo wanted to share it. He stretched out his fingers and put his whole heart into the first bright chords of Miss Ella's tune.

As Leo's hands marched through the tune, everyone turned to Miss Ella with sweet astonishment. She sang for all to hear, and soon the room filled with joyful voices. Leo was sharing his treasure. A gift for Miss Ella—and everyone—just in time for Christmas.

"Play it again," said Miss Ella.

And Leo did.

Hark! The Herald Angels Sing

C. Wesley

Felix Mendelssohn (1809–1847)

Hark! The he - rald an - gels sing, "Glo - ry to the new - born King;

Peace on earth, and mer - cy mild God and sin - ners rec - on - ciled!" Joy - ful, all ye

na - tions, rise, Join the tri - umph of the skies; With th'an - gel - ic host pro - claim,

"Christ is born in Beth - le - hem!" Hark! the he - rald an - gels sing, "Glo - ry to the new - born King;

"Hark! The Herald Angels Sing" is a work in the public domain. This work is the result of multiple adaptations of a hymn written by Charles Wesley in 1739. The carol familiar to us today is an adaptation of an 1840 cantata of Felix Mendelssohn arranged to fit the lyrics.

Book jacket author photo credits (top to bottom): Jone MacCulloch, Warling Studios, Kathryn Seckman Kirsch.

ISBN: 978-0-8294-4600-5

Library of Congress Control Number: 2017946212

Printed in the United States of America

17 18 19 20 21 22 23 24 25 26 Bang 10 9 8 7 6 5 4 3 2 1

LOYOLA PRESS.
3441 N. Ashland Avenue
Chicago, Illinois 60657
(800) 621-1008
www.loyolapress.com